Chapter II *Little* IVB '84
84

S

When Everyone Was Fast Asleep

When Everyone
Was Fast Asleep

WRITTEN AND ILLUSTRATED BY

Tomie de Paola

PUFFIN BOOKS

FOR
MAXINE
&
DOUGLE·BEADS

First published by Holiday House 1976
Published in Picture Puffins 1979

Copyright © 1976 by Tomie de Paola

Library of Congress Cataloging in Publication Data
De Paola, Thomas Anthony.   When everyone was fast asleep.
Summary: When everyone was fast asleep, the Fog
Maiden sent a cat to carry two sleeping children off
for a fantastical evening highlighted by a palace ball.
[1. Fantasy.   2.   Night—Fiction] I. Title.
PZ7.D439Wh 1979   [E]   79-560
ISBN 0 14 050.310 2

When everyone was fast asleep,
the Fog Maiden sent Token to wake us up.

And we slid
through the curtains
into the night.

We floated
across the grass,
dancing on the dew,
and met the elf horse.

We all sang,
"Tra la, tra la,
too lay, too lay,
hop-a-doodle,
hip-a-doodle,
flip-a-doodle day."

Down the road we went,
counting moons
until we came
to the troll house,
but we were not afraid.

We ate
hot buttered bread
and drank
warm milk with honey,

And dressed for the ball at the palace.

The crocodiles
danced a quadrille
and the peacocks
waltzed with doves
and we all sang,
"Tra la, tra la,
too lay, too lay,
hop-a-doodle,
hip-a-doodle,
flip-a-doodle day."

When the king
and queen arrived,
the play began.

The lion roared
while the gypsy slept,

And the princess
was saved by
the sand serpent.

The night was over
and the Fog Maiden came
to cover everything
with her dress.

She picked us up
and floated
over the trees
to our very own window,

Where she tucked us
into our beds
and kissed us asleep.

EGNAR PUBLIC SCHOOL
BOX 37
EGNAR, COLORADO 81325